I0784069

GOOD SPORTS

Dale Lazarov & Alessio Slonimsky

GOOD SPORTS

Script and art direction by Dale Lazarov
Linework and colors by Alessio Slonimsky
©2012 Dale Lazarov & Alessio Slonimsky // All rights reserved.

StickyGraphicNovels.com

Printed and distributed by
ComicMix, LLC.,
304 Main Avenue, Suite #194,
Norwalk, CT 06851.
http://www.comicmix.com

Printed in USA.

Hardcover ISBN: 978-1-939888-52-5

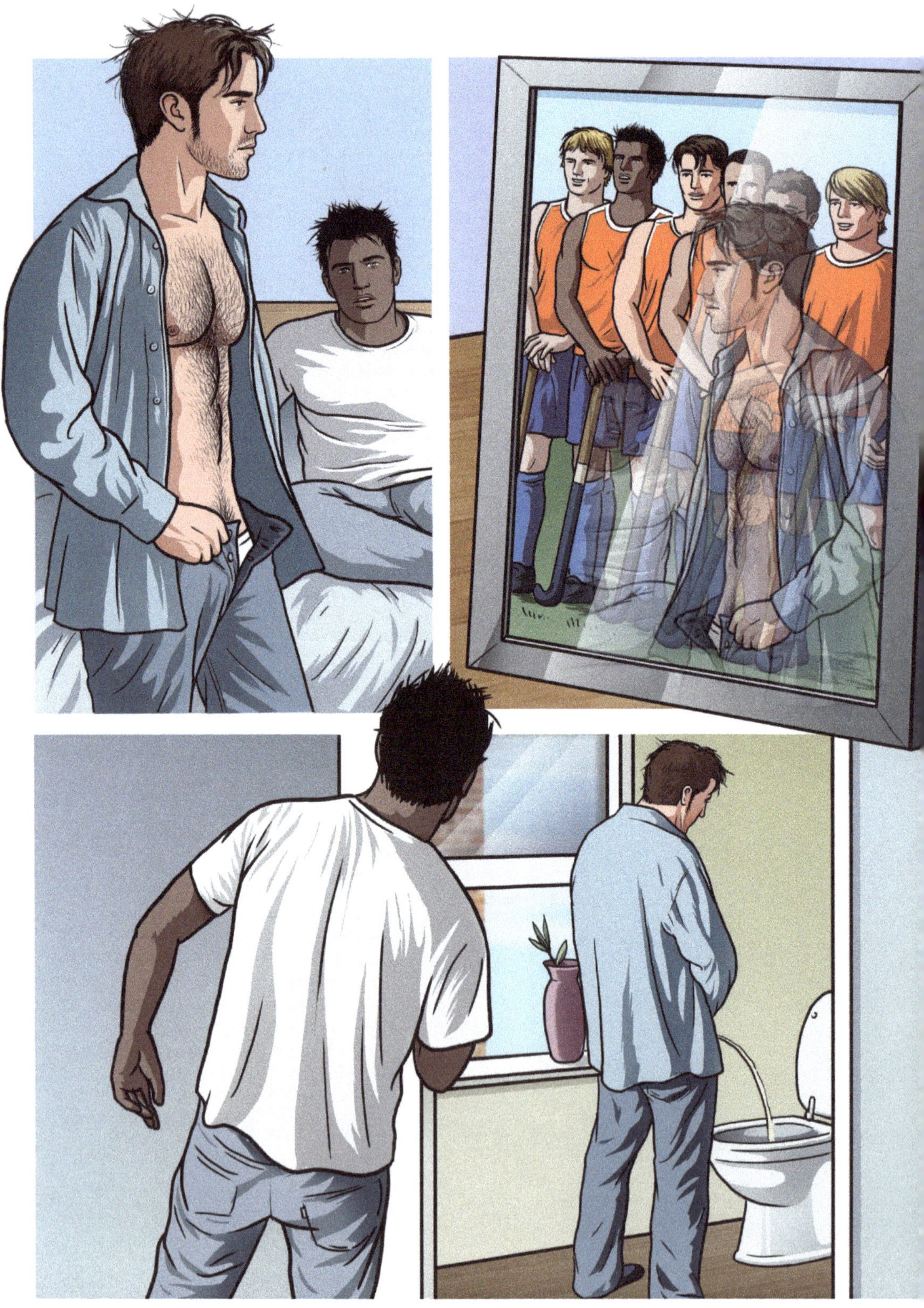

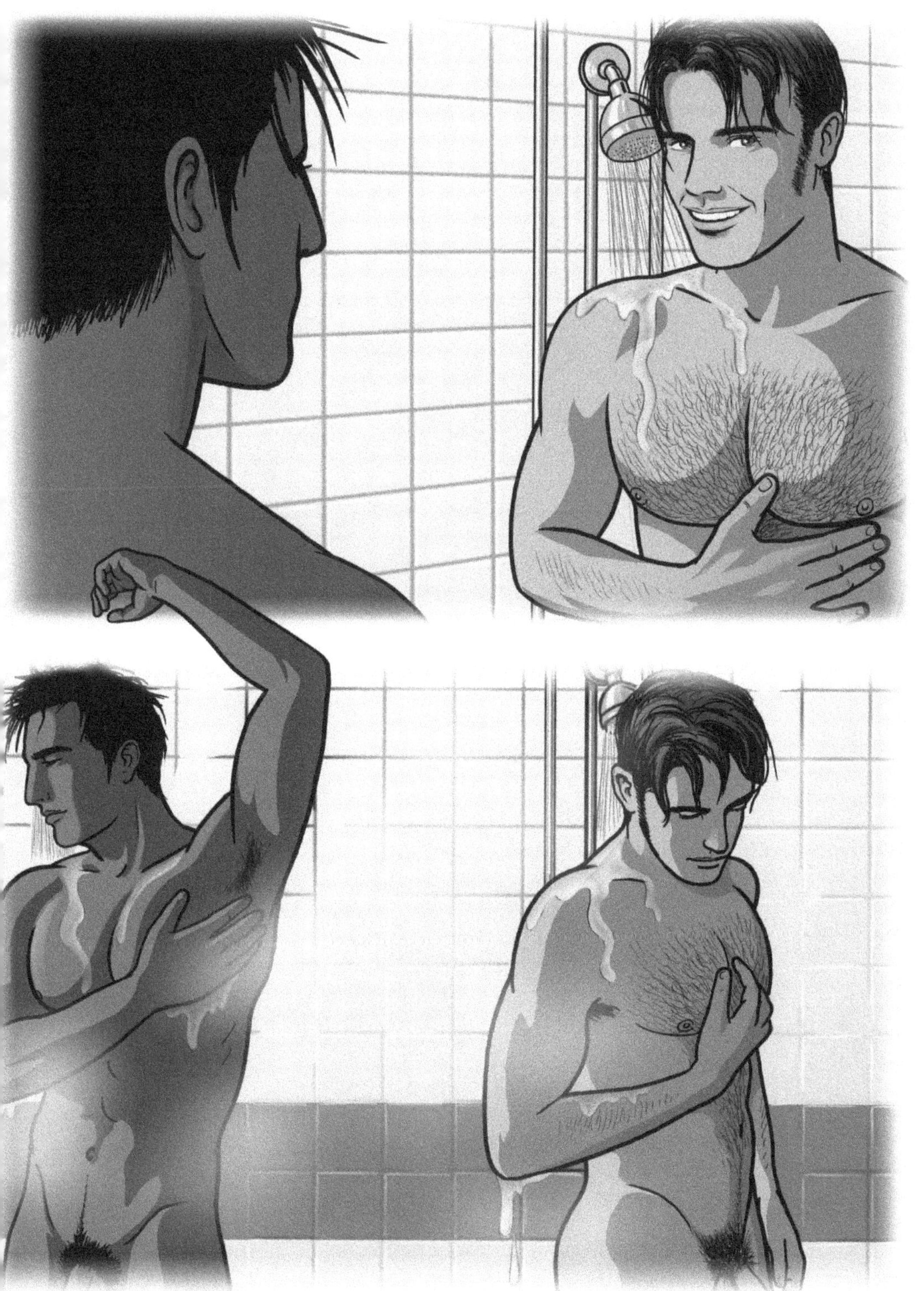

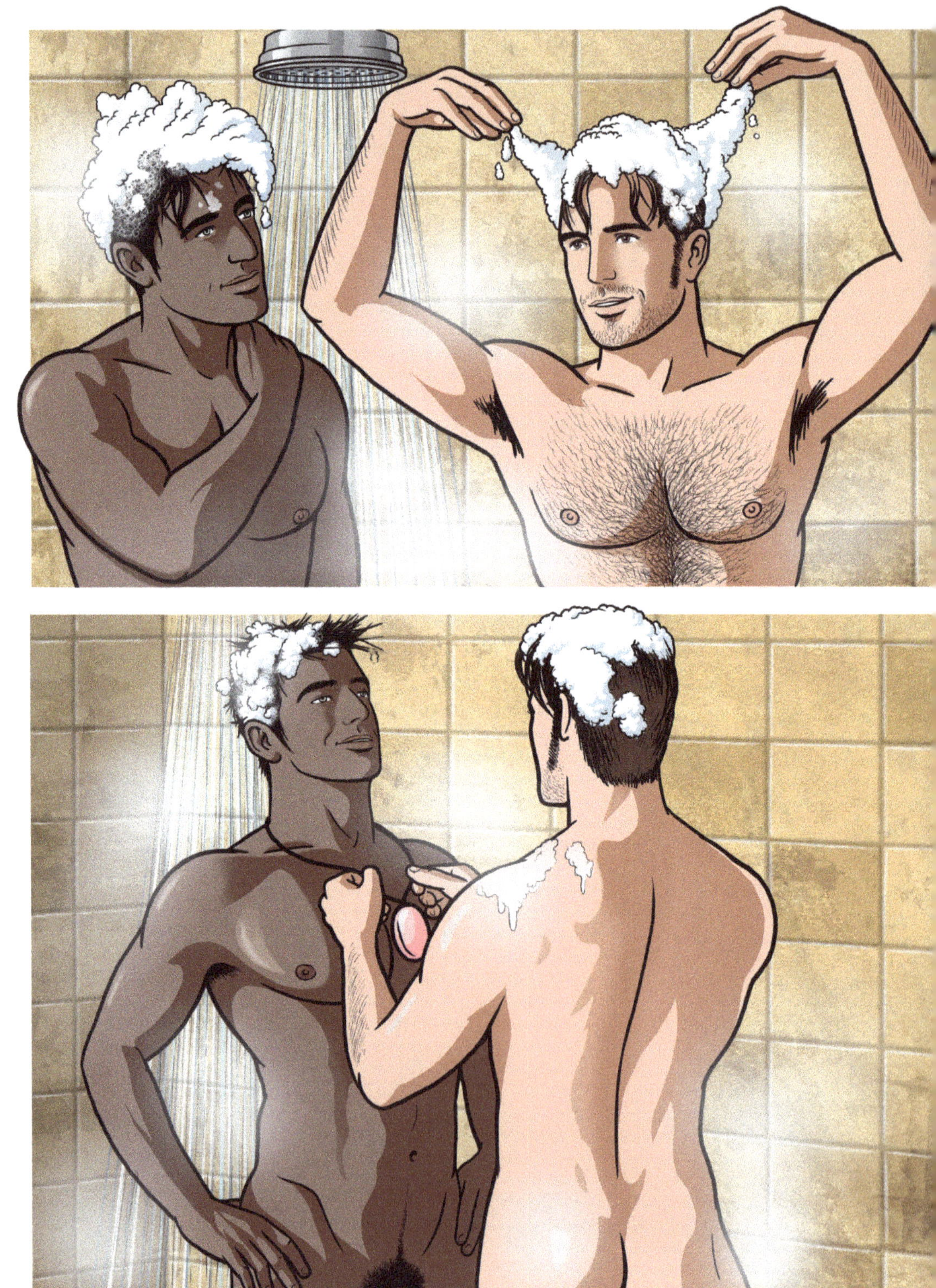

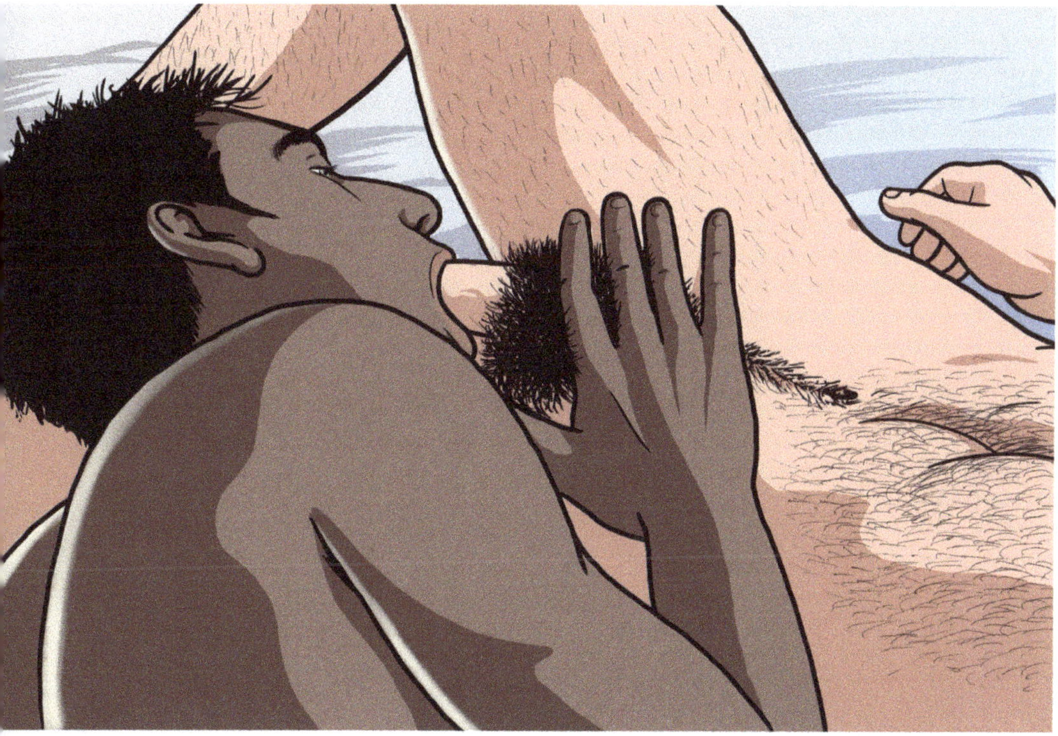

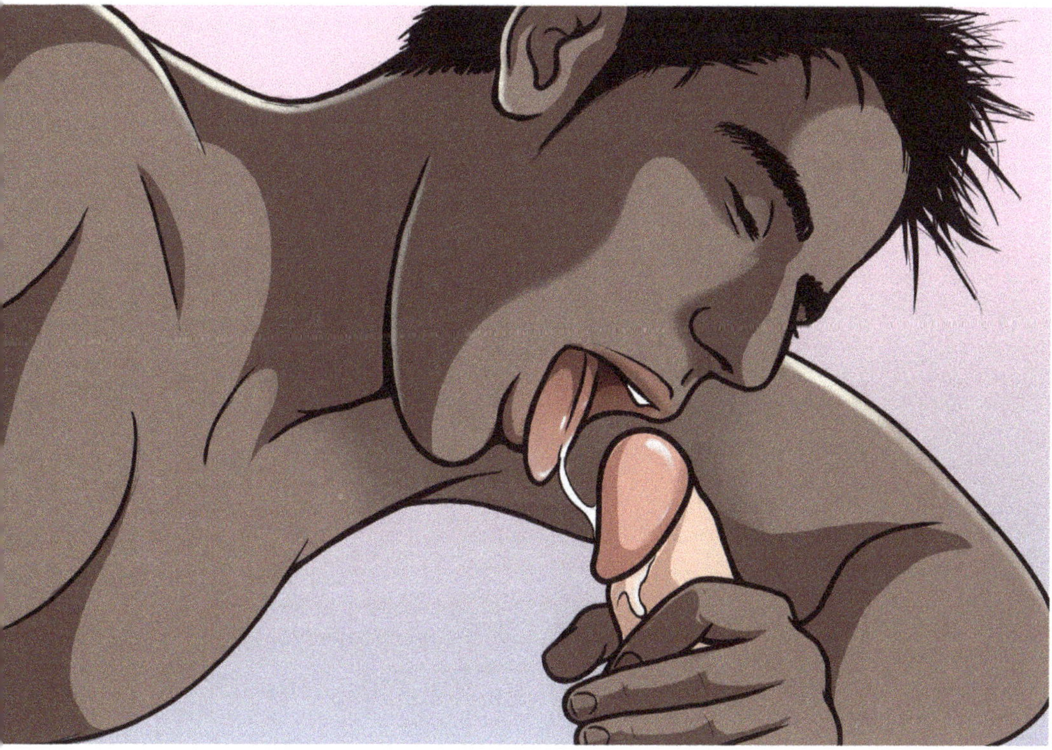

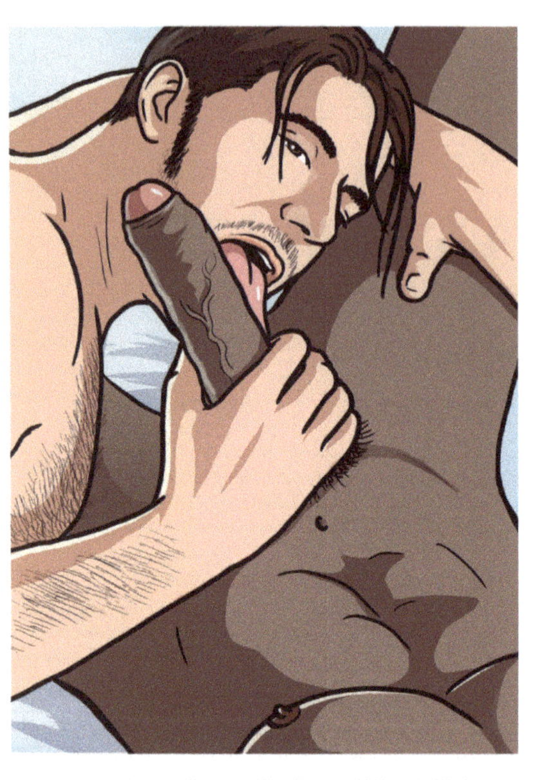
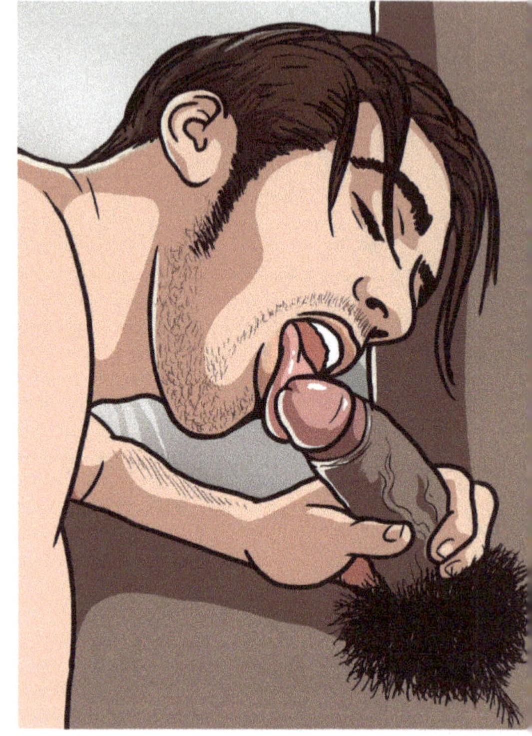
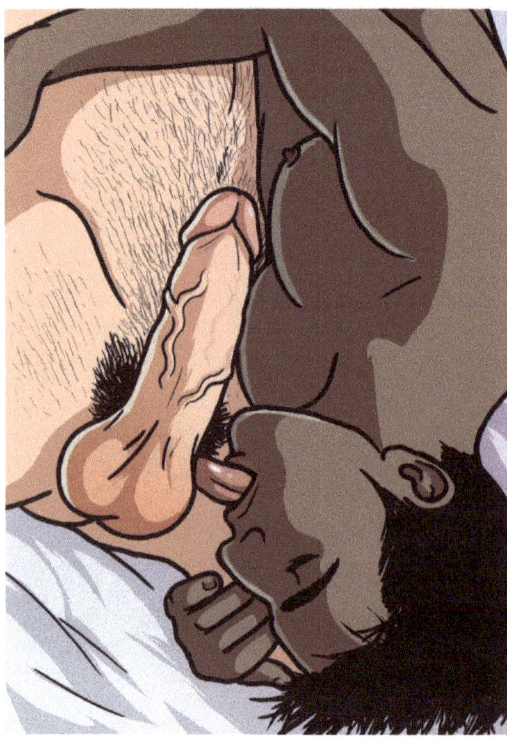

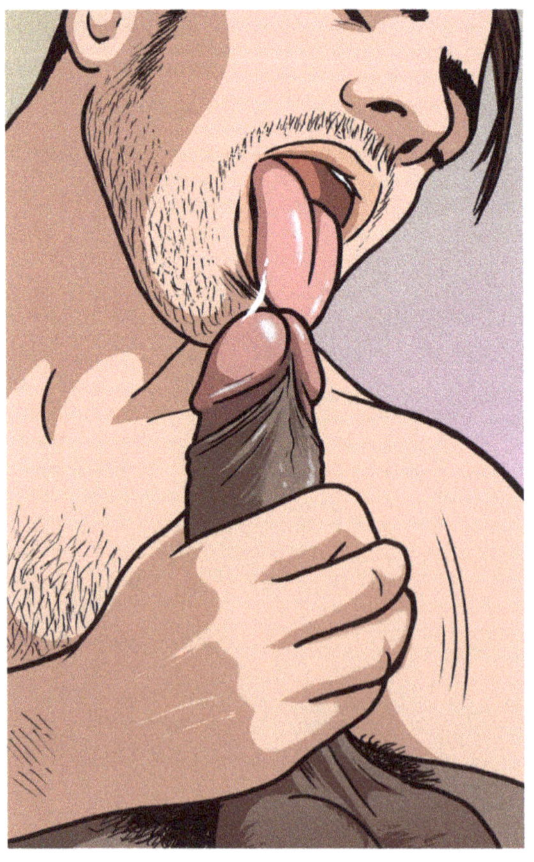
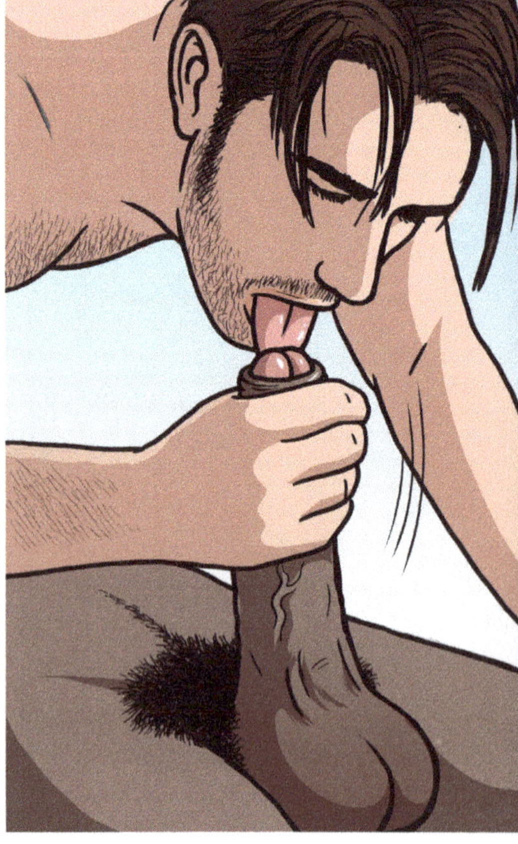

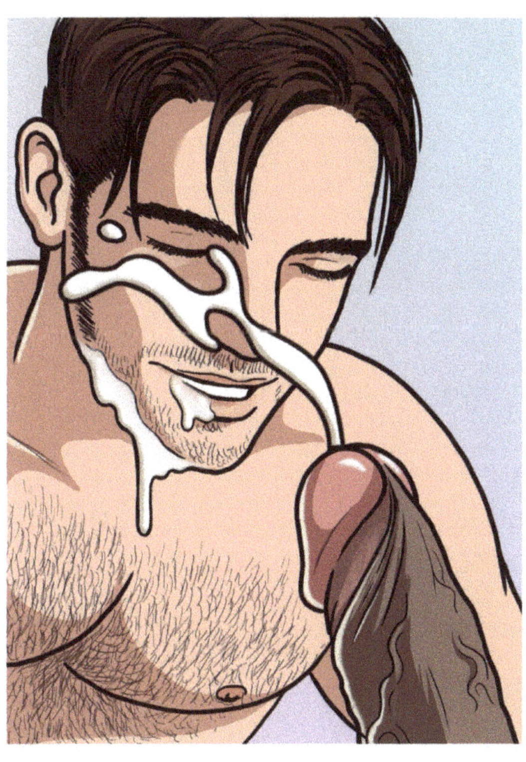

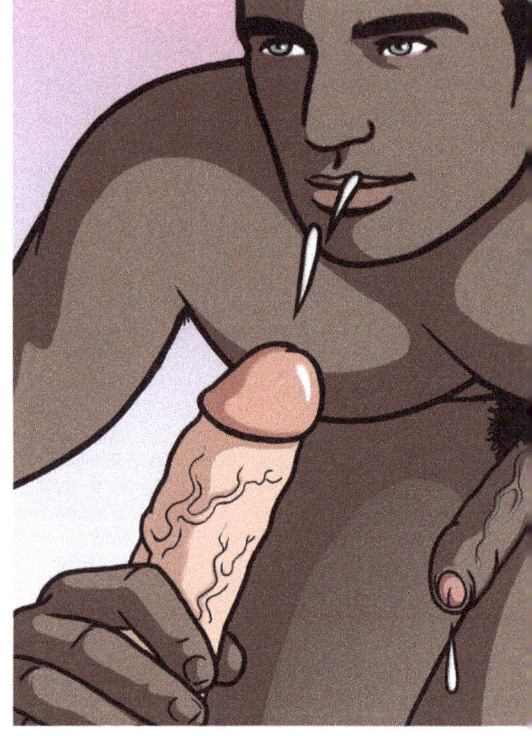

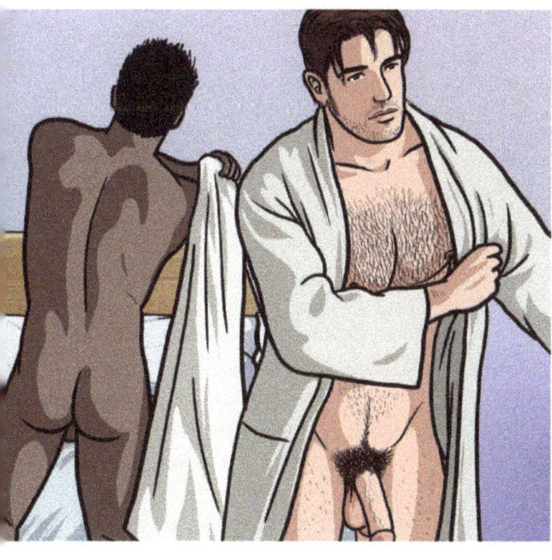

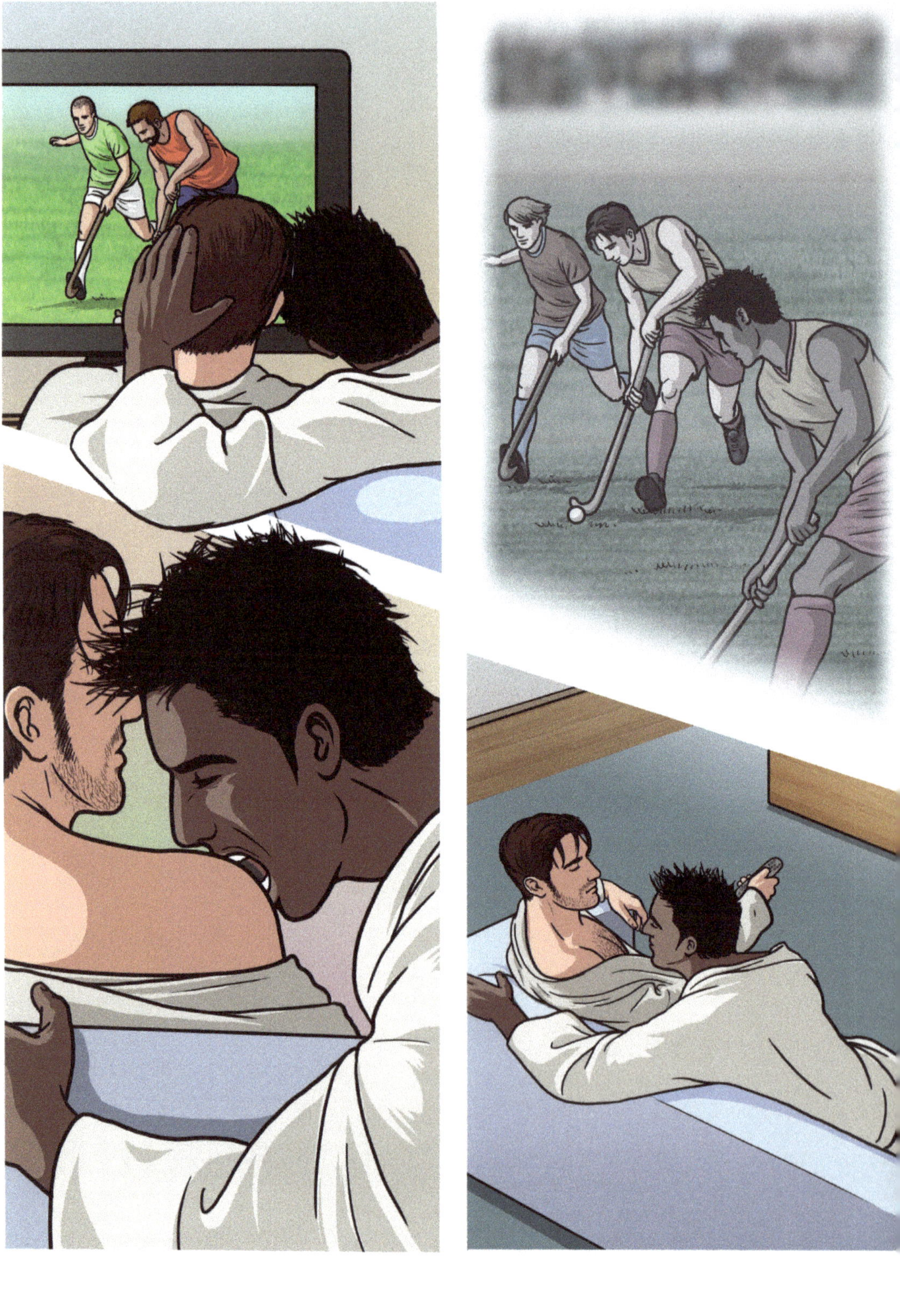

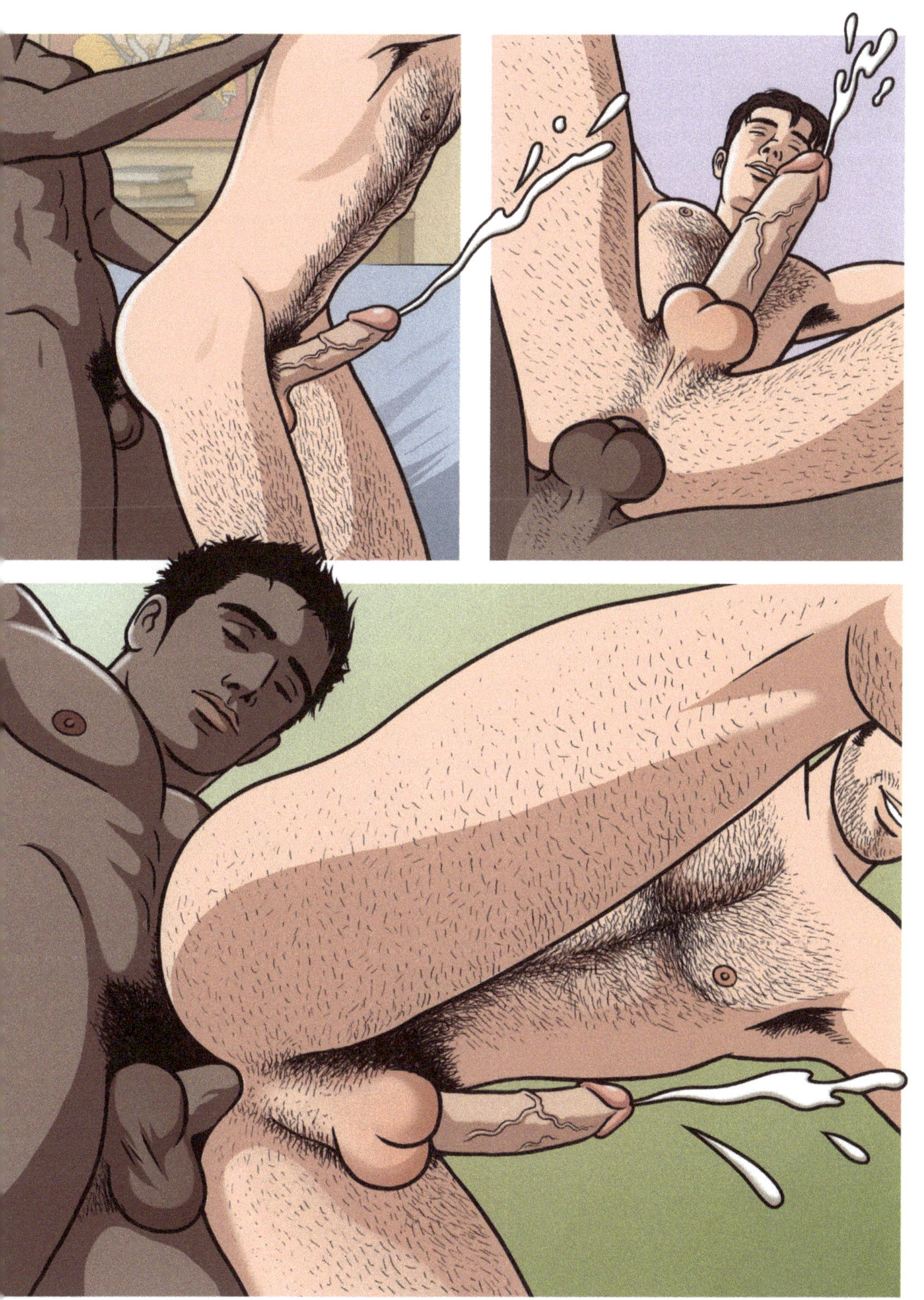

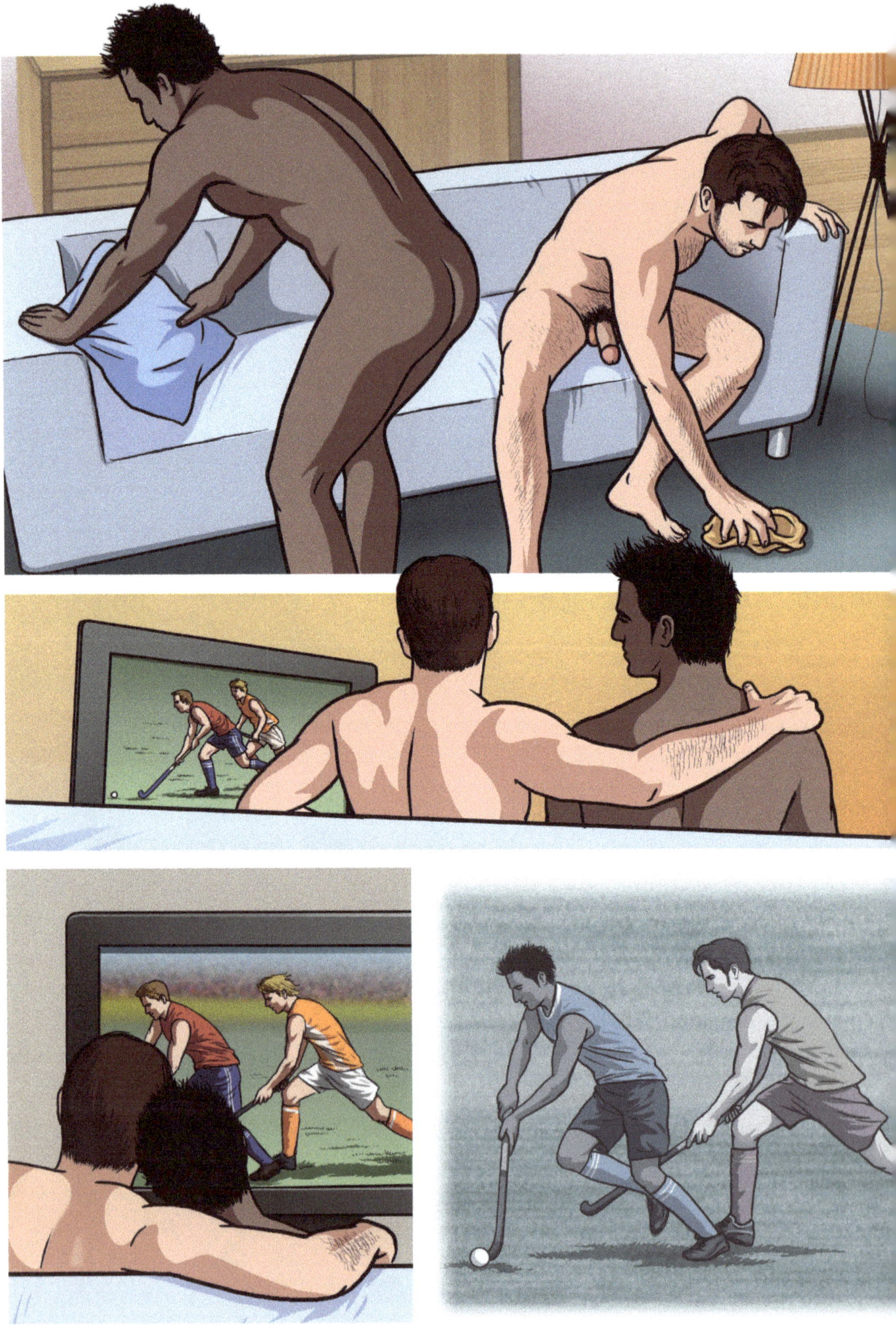

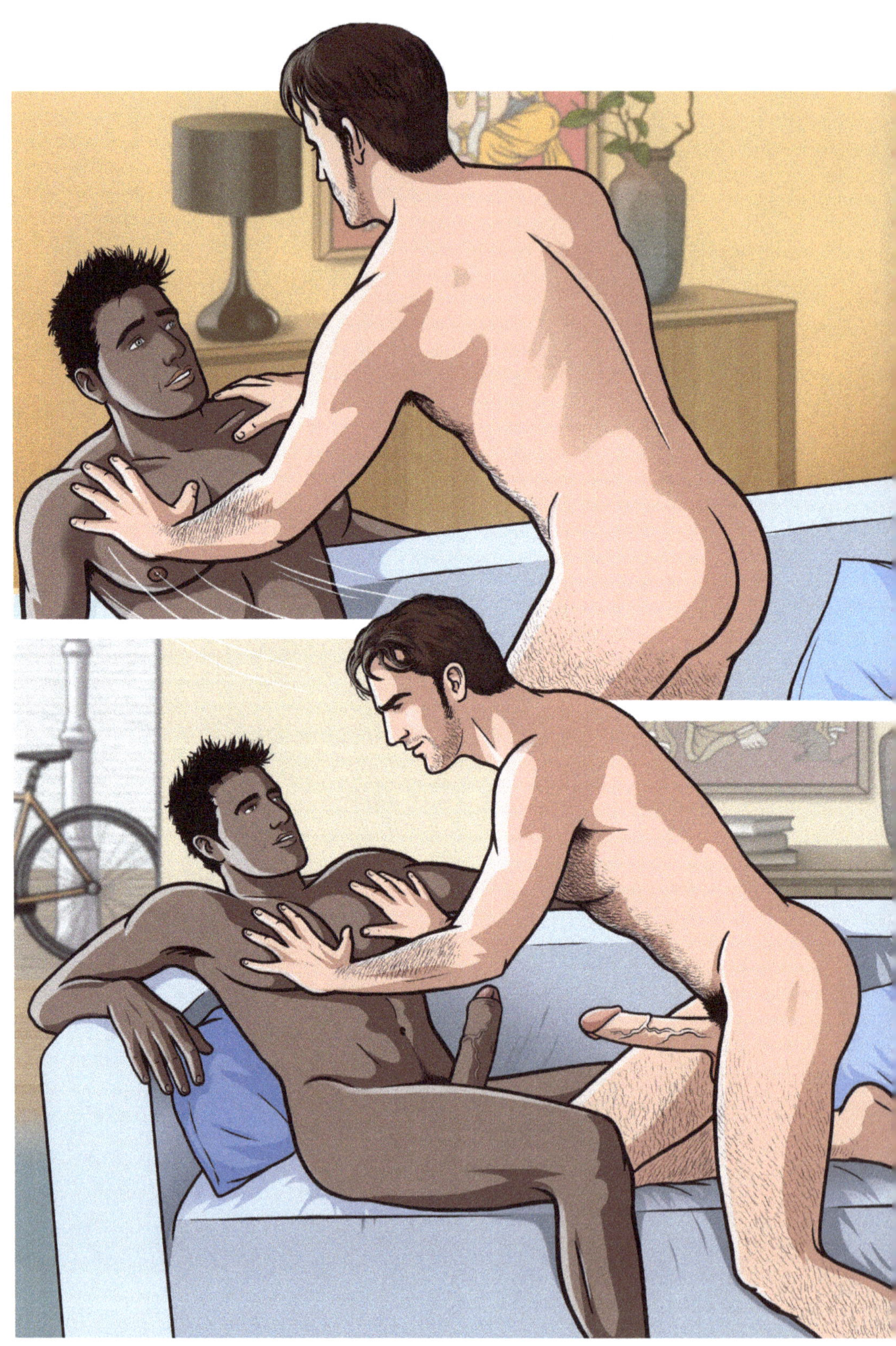

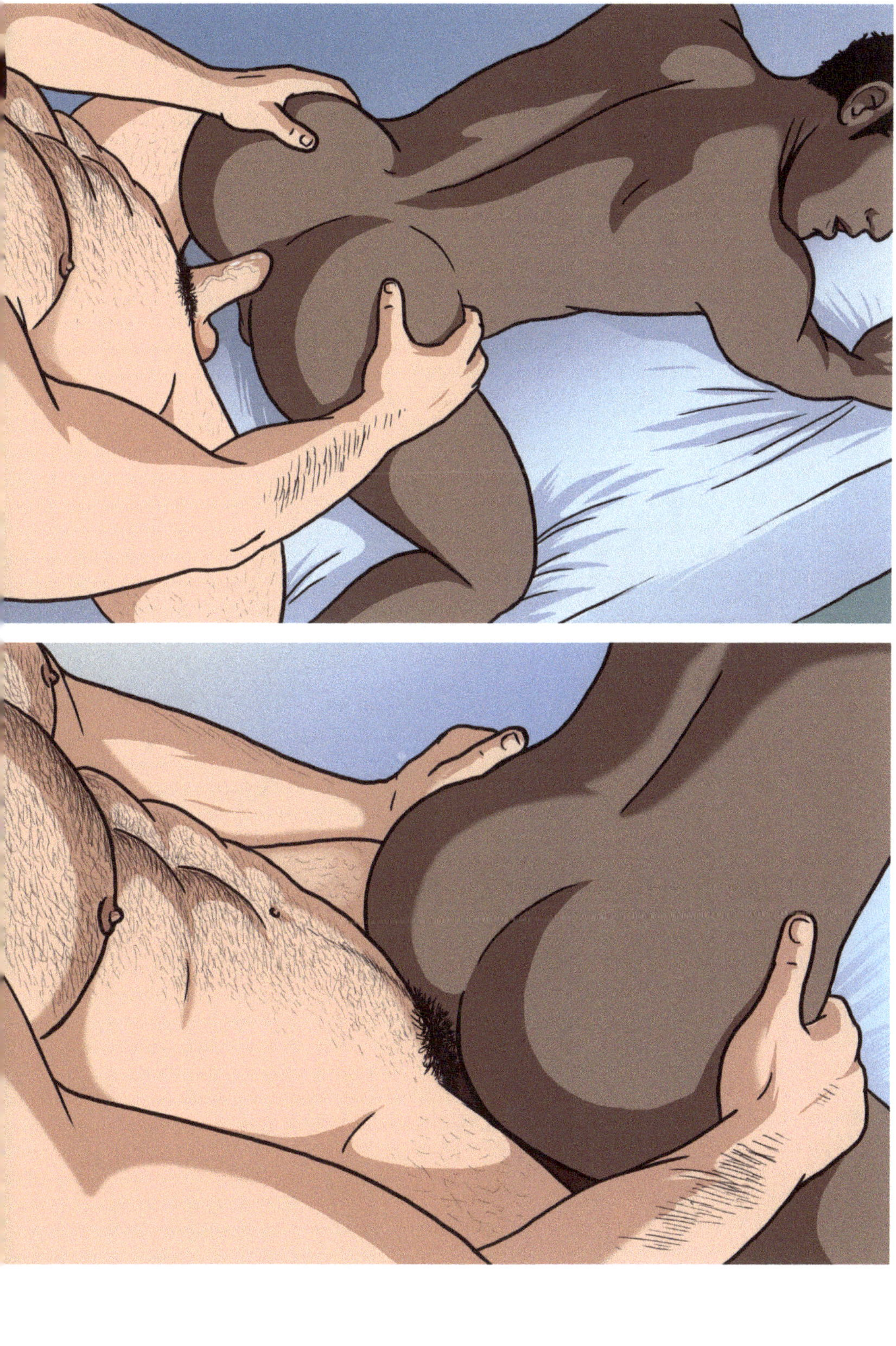

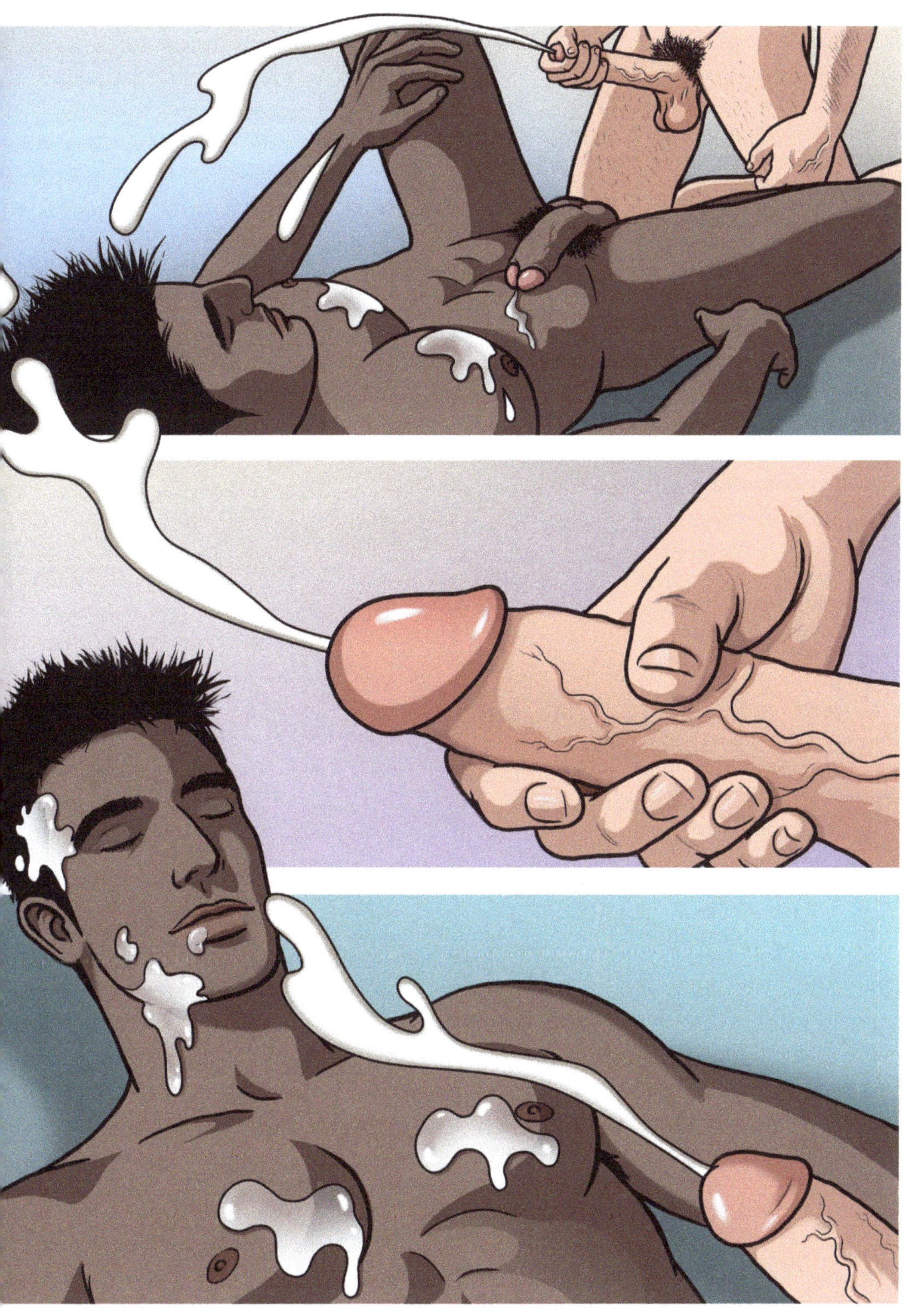

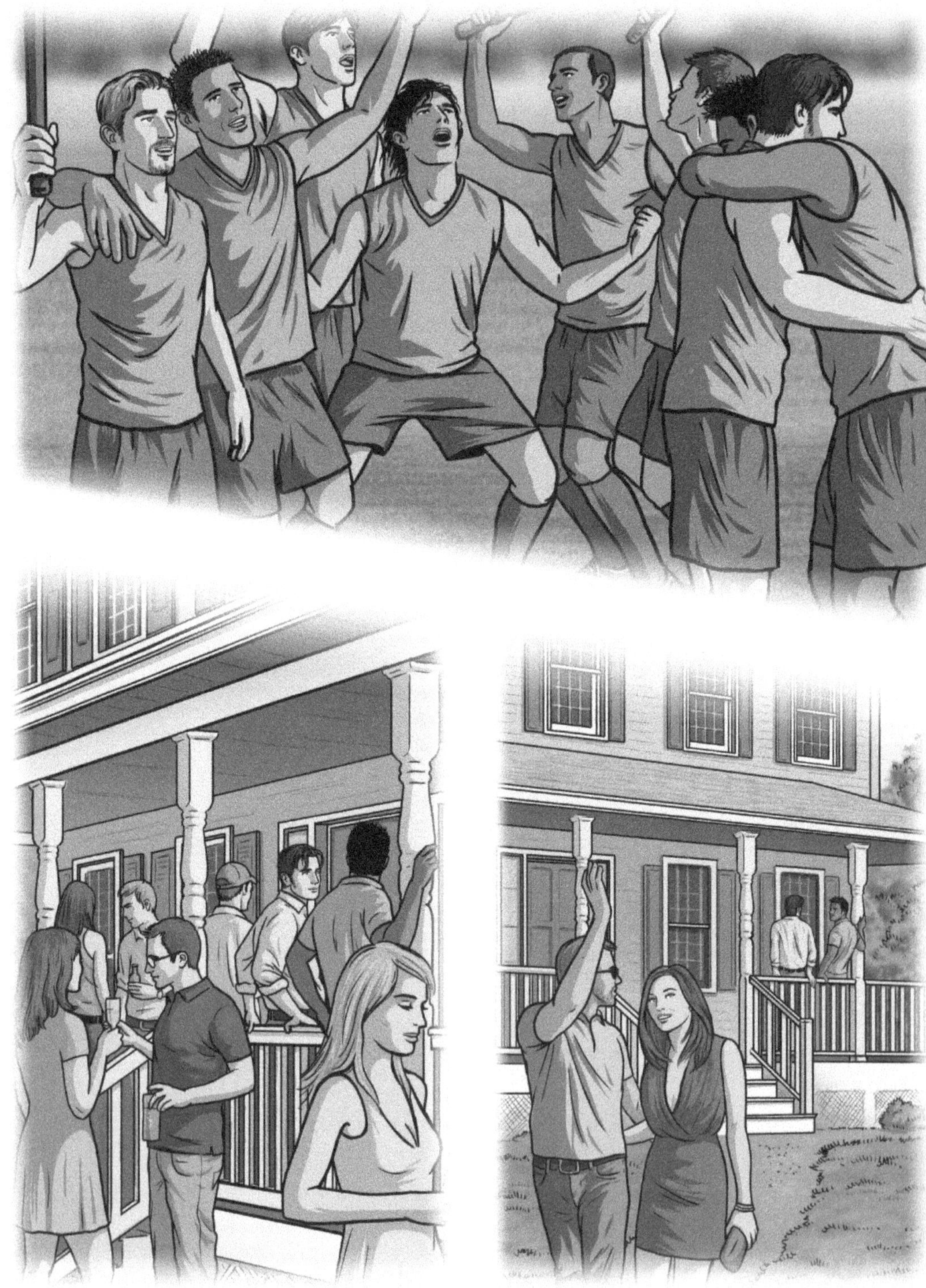

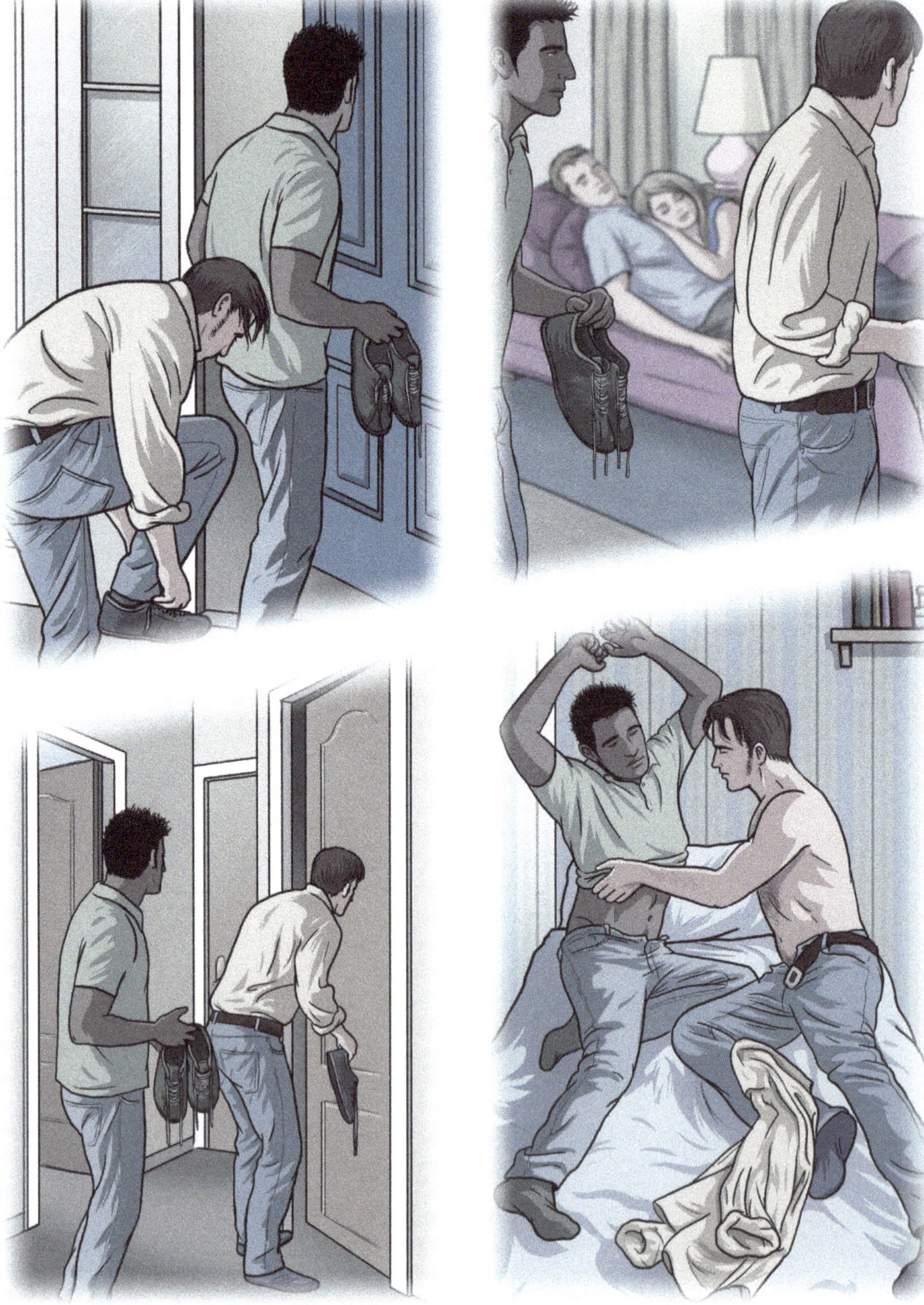

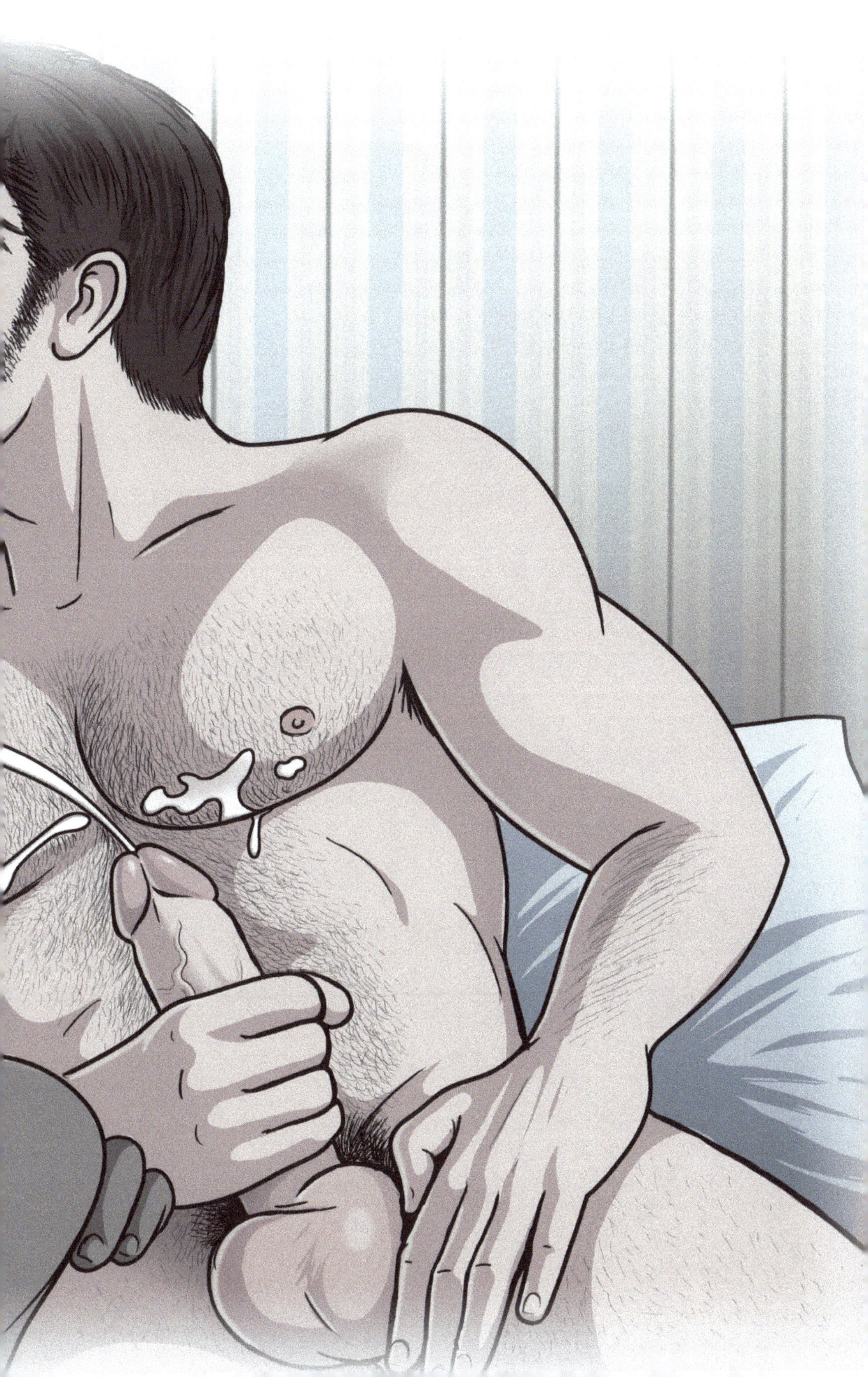

THE
END

GOOD SPORTS
script/edits: Dale Lazarov
art: Alessio Slonimsky

About The Authors:

<u>Dale Lazarov</u> is the writer/art director of TIMBER (drawn by Player), SLY (drawn by mpMann), BULLDOGS (drawn by Chas Hunter & Si Arden), PARDNERS (drawn by Bo Revel), PEACOCK PUNKS (drawn by Mauro Mariotti), FAST FRIENDS (drawn by Michael Broderick), GREEK LOVE (drawn by Adam Graphite), GOOD SPORTS (drawn by Alessio Slonimsky), NIGHTLIFE (drawn by Bastian Jonsson), MANLY (drawn by Amy Colburn), and STICKY (drawn by Steve MacIsaac) —wordless, gay character-based, sex-positive graphic novels published in hardcover by ComicMix and in digital format through Class Comics. He lives in Chicago.

<u>Alessio Slonimsky</u> comes from an artistic family and has been drawing from an early age. He majored in Fine Arts in Spain and received his MFA in illustration in New York City. After working for advertising agencies and publishing companies as a freelance illustrator, he began publishing erotic comics and illustrations on the internet in 2009. His website is at alessioinwonderland.blogspot.com.

www.ingramcontent.com/pod-product-compliance
Lightning Source LLC
Chambersburg PA
CBHW041553010826
48981CB00045B/188